by Meish Goldish • illustrated by Michael Reid

SCHOLASTIC INC.
New York   Toronto   London   Auckland   Sydney
Mexico City   New Delhi   Hong Kong   Buenos Aires

Developed by Kirchoff/Wohlberg, Inc., in cooperation with Scholastic Inc.

The Case of the Strange Noise

Ken and Mike were playing in their house. Suddenly they heard a loud noise.

"What was that?" Ken asked.

"I'm not sure," Mike said. "It sounds like a bird chirping."

"Maybe a bird is outside," Ken said.

The boys went back to playing their game. A minute later, they heard the noise again.

"It does sound like a bird," Mike agreed. "But it sounds like it's inside our house. We don't have a bird."

"Let's get Gail," Ken said.

They went next door to the Smart home. Gail answered the door.

"Hey, guys. What's up?" she asked. "How can I help you?"

"We can hear a strange noise at our house," Mike said. "We think it may be a bird, but we're not sure."

Gail pulled a card out of her pocket. She handed it to the boys. It read:

Gail Smart,
Kid Detective

I Can Solve Any Mystery.

No Emergency Too Great or Too Small.

"I'm on the case," said Gail.

The three children entered the boys' home. The chirping noise sounded again.

"If it's a bird, it had to come through an open window or door," Gail said. She looked around the house with Ken and Mike. All the windows and doors were closed.

Just then, they heard the chirp again. Gail pointed to a closet. "It sounds like it came from inside there," she announced to her friends.

"Don't open the closet door," Ken warned. "The bird might be a big one."

Gail sat on the floor to think. What was that noise?

4

After a minute, the chirp sounded again.

"I don't think it's a bird," Gail said. She looked at her watch and began counting softly to herself.

Ken said, "Gail, what are you do—"

"Shhh!" Gail said, cutting him off. "I think the noise is about to sound again. Five, four, three, two, one."

Sure enough, at that moment, another chirp came from the closet.

"Where is your mom?" Gail asked.

"She's out buying some batteries," said Ken.

"Now I know what's in the closet," Gail said. She opened the door. On a shelf lay a smoke alarm. Suddenly, it chirped loudly.

"That's our spare smoke alarm," Ken said. "In case our regular one breaks."

"Yes," Gail said. "And when its battery runs low, the alarm chirps as a warning. Your mom must be getting a new battery for it. There's no bird here."

"How did you know?" Ken asked, "It sounded like one."

"The chirps were exactly sixty seconds apart. A bird wouldn't chirp that way."

"Gail does it again!" the boys cried.

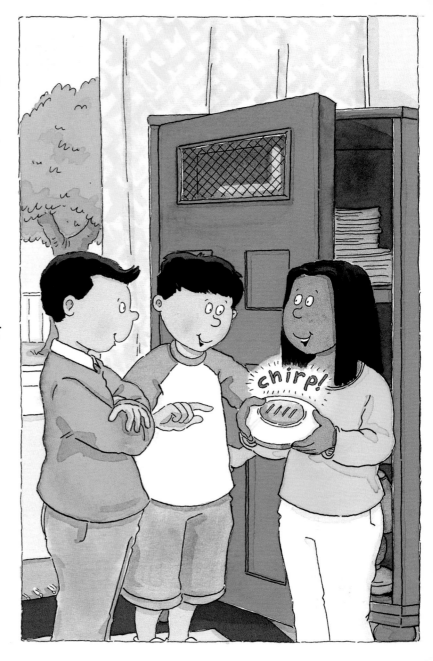

The Case of the Missing Pet

Ken and Mike were playing in their yard. They saw a caterpillar crawling in the grass. Ken picked it up with a twig. The caterpillar didn't seem to mind.

"This can be our new pet!" Ken cried.

The boys went inside and placed the caterpillar in a shoebox. They lined the box with leaves and grass for the caterpillar to eat. They put in twigs for it to crawl on. Then they put the lid on the box.

"Let's punch holes in the lid," said Mike. "That way, the caterpillar can breathe."

Every day, the boys looked inside the box. They lifted the lid and watched the caterpillar crawl on the twigs.

Then one day, the boys looked inside the box. The caterpillar was not there!

"Maybe it crawled out," Ken said.

The boys searched all around the box. They checked on the floor and under the table. There was no sign of the caterpillar.

"This is a mystery for Gail to solve," Mike said. "She's a great detective. She'll know how to find our missing caterpillar."

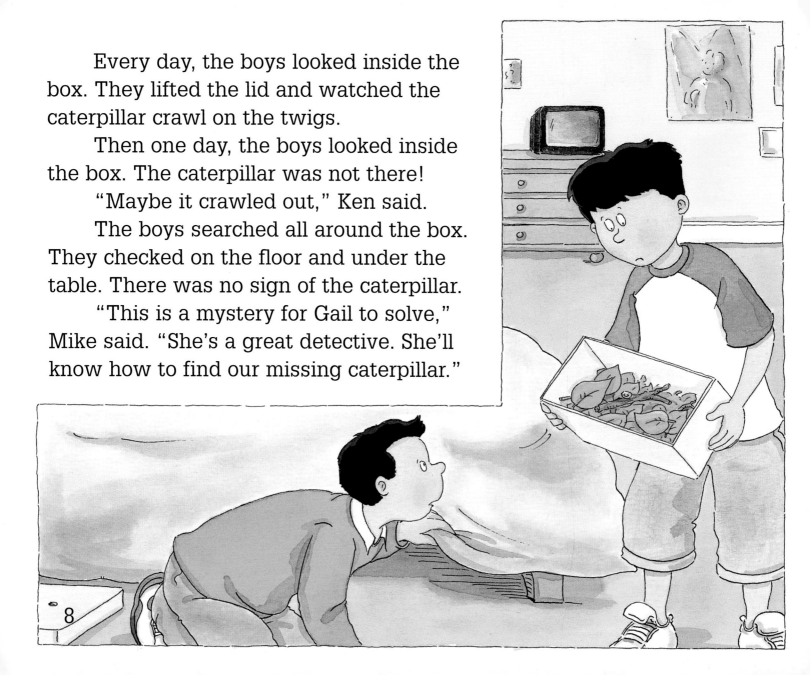

8

Ken called Gail on the telephone and explained the emergency. She came over right away. She studied the shoebox lid.

"Did you keep the lid on at all times?" Gail asked.

"We only took it off to watch our caterpillar crawl," Mike explained.

Gail looked at the lid again. "I don't think the caterpillar could have crawled through these holes. They're too small."

Then Gail looked inside the box. She saw something like a shell hanging from one of the twigs.

"Was this shell always here?" Gail asked.

"I don't think so," Ken said.

"Neither do I," said Mike.

Gail asked, "Could I please have a glass of hot water? And put an ice cube in it."

Mike looked surprised, but he brought Gail what she asked for. Gail pointed to the ice. The three children watched it slowly melt.

"What does this prove?" Mike asked.

"Things don't always stay the same," Gail said. "Sometimes they change their form."

"What do you mean?" asked Ken.

"Your caterpillar isn't missing," Gail explained. "It's just changing its form, like the ice cube. Please cover the shoebox for another couple of weeks. Then look and see what's inside."

After waiting a week, the boys lifted the shoebox lid. Out flew a beautiful butterfly!

"A caterpillar forms a hard shell. Then it turns into a butterfly," Gail explained. "I already knew that. Now, so do you."

"Gail solves another case!" the boys cried.

The Case of the Late-Night Reader

Ken and Mike went to Gail's house for a sleep-over.

"This will be fun," said Ken. "We can stay up all night and read lots of books."

Gail shook her head. "You can stay up until my mom says it's time for lights out," she said. "You cannot stay up all night, though. If you did, you'd be much too tired the next day. That's just common sense."

"But we like to read all night," said Mike.

"Not in my home," said Gail.

That night, the three played games until nine o'clock. Then they brushed their teeth.

"Now it's time for bed," Gail's mom said. "All lights must be out."

Ken and Mike slept in beds in the guest room. Each bed had a little silver night lamp next to it.

Gail's room was across the hall. From her bed, she could see a light shining under the boys' door. She left her room and knocked on their door. Suddenly, she heard a lamp click off. The boys' room went dark suddenly.

"Time for bed," Gail said.

Gail returned to her room and climbed into bed. After a minute, she saw the light under the boys' door appear again. Gail left her room and knocked on their door. Again, she suddenly heard a lamp click off. The boys' room grew dark again.

"I really mean it this time," Gail said. "No reading now. It's bedtime."

"I wasn't reading," said Ken. "Really!"

"I wasn't reading," said Mike. "Really!"

"One of you was reading," Gail said. "Or maybe both of you. Now, go to sleep."

Gail got back in her bed. Just then, she saw the light go on under the boys' door.

"This time I'll surprise them," Gail thought. She got out of bed and walked to their door. As she was about to turn the knob, the light under the door went out.

Gail opened the door quickly. She turned on the overhead light.

"Which one of you was reading?" she asked.

"Not me," said Ken.

"Not me," said Mike.

Gail noticed a book near Mike's pillow.

Gail looked at Mike. "I'll bet anything it was you who was reading," she said to him.

"No, it wasn't," Mike insisted. "You can't prove that. You're not that smart."

"I'm a great detective and can solve this case," said Gail.

She walked over to the night lamps by the boys' beds. She felt each light bulb.

"Mike, your light bulb is warm. Ken, yours is not. That proves Mike was reading."

"Gail solves another case!" the boys cried. Everyone slept the rest of the night. They woke up rested.